PROJECT DOME

A NOVELETTE ABOUT SCIENCE AND THE HUMAN TRAGEDY

T. D. CHASE

CONTENTS

1. One Is The Loneliest Number   7
2. Hello Darkness   11
3. Table For Six   14
4. Green Eggs and Ham   18
5. I Robot   22
6. Let's Get Ready To Rumble   24
7. Down With The Sickness   27
8. Time Is On My Side   29

   About the Author   31
   Also by T. D. Chase   33

For Professor Tom Nash
You are the reason this book exists.

BLURB

PROJECT DOME
A NOVELETTE ABOUT SCIENCE AND THE
HUMAN TRAGEDY

Climb aboard The Project Dome.

Decide for yourself if you want to survive the unimaginable.

CHAPTER 1
ONE IS THE LONELIEST NUMBER

I remember it all so clearly, like it was yesterday. It wasn't supposed to happen for at least another fifteen to fifty years. Stars like our sun are supposed to last nine or ten billion years. To say they did not prepare us on Earth for this event was an understatement. We didn't even come close. Most of the population still didn't believe that our sun was on its way out. Most of the population figured it was just another scheme to get people to save energy, save the ozone layer, or recycle more. Despite the announcement from the top scientists' in the world, many still didn't believe our sun could be dying.

I remember the day the World Leader verified the terrible rumors. Though he downplayed the harsh reality with promises of underground safety. Along with reassurances that dome type structures would be in place to house the population. He also assured the people that there is plenty of time left to get these things in place. Why anyone would want to live through such a catastrophe was a matter few seemed to address. I remember the attitude seemed to be that it simply wasn't real and if it was, 'they' would fix it before anything life changing could happen.

Earth's sun burning out wasn't something anyone could fix, except for God. It didn't look like He was going to intervene, and He didn't. The signs were there that this event was going to, in fact, take place. Even with the cooling temperatures and the sun flickering, people just went about their lives. Everyone continued acting like nothing so utterly devastating, and life ending was coming. But coming it was, and much sooner than anyone expected.

Like I mentioned, there were supposed to be many dome-like structures built that would house several thousand people each, for approximately one hundred years. That was the plan, but we didn't get started soon enough. The scientists had predicted the sun would first use up the hydrogen that keeps it burning. Then, it would go through the phases of star death. But that isn't exactly how it went down.

On this particular day, myself and five other

scientists were working in Dome One, trying to figure out the glitch in the water system. This unit was to house five hundred people, but future domes were going to have a capacity of housing several thousand. Looking back on things, I question why we would want to survive such an apocalyptic event. I guess it's because it's what we do as human beings. We must go on.

The six of us had been working most of the day. We had just figured out why the water system wasn't working properly and we were getting ready to head home for the day when it happened. The sun started flickering, going dim, then bright, dim, then bright. We were standing in the main room at the entrance of the dome. It is a giant room of mostly windows, which are huge panels of unbreakable glass like material. None of us said anything. We just stood there and watched outside at what was taking place.

The flickering sun was still going from dim to bright, but the dimness was lasting longer each time. Something was definitely happening. What we didn't know. Then the flickering stopped, and it was like it was late afternoon again. We collectively let out our breaths. We were all feeling a little shaky, and we all started talking over each other. Nervous with relief, and that's when the unimaginable happened. The sun flicked off for the last time. Boom. We stood there looking up into the strangest sight. The sun was a dark mass, but the day still looked sunny. Then, from somewhere came the reality into my brain. The light from the burned out sun was still traveling. When the last of the traveling light reached us, utter complete blackness was going to be beyond the dome walls.

CHAPTER 2
HELLO DARKNESS

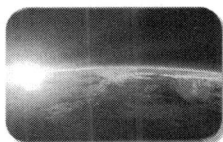

N o one said anything, for I don't know how long. Our brains were struggling to process what had just happened. Then, instinct told me I needed to get to the panel at the entrance of the dome and get it locked. I started running just as I heard a noise outside getting louder by the second. I could feel and hear whatever made that noise outside! Deep down on some level, I knew what the noise was. But I was still running on instinct. Then, the reality of the moment slammed into my head. I had to get to the panel and lock the entrance to the dome before the hordes of people who were racing to the dome could get there. Because if I wasn't able to lock the entrance, then we would all die.

Those on the other side of the dome walls when the sun finally burned out were already dead. That meant everyone outside was lost. Men, women and children, walking, or running, were dead. I hit the panel seconds before the masses reached the dome. The six of us stood in silence as the chaos took place. The hordes of people were pounding and screaming at the walls and the door of the dome, demanding to be let in. We couldn't let them in. Oh, there was room inside the dome, but if we let them in, we all would die.

Everyone had to go through a sterilization process before you could enter the dome. A process that took five minutes. We could have let four hundred and ninety-four more into the building, twenty at a time. But the scared, panicked people outside wouldn't have counted off twenty and stopped. They would have rushed in at once in a massive stampede, and we didn't have the power to prevent them. Listening to the shouting and pleading people was agony for us. The only saving grace was that we couldn't see anyone through the windows after eight minutes. It was pitch black outside. It took eight minutes for the light from the sun to reach us after the sun burned out. In that eight minutes we saw our friends, colleagues and, worst of all, our families outside begging to be let in. To make matters worse, we had to endure this for days. It took several days for the Earth's temperature to cool to no longer sustain life anymore.

I've reflected on why we didn't prepare sooner for this so we could have saved more people. And then I think, saved for what? For life inside a dome module? I know why they didn't announce it sooner, if in fact they knew. After watching what some people were capable of outside while they were trying to get in, it gave me an idea of what people might have done if they knew there could be no long-term consequences.

Perhaps we thought we might be rescued by another life form somewhere down the frozen road. This is the only reason I can come up with to willingly, proactively make sure to survive a disaster of this magnitude. But stay alive we did, by keeping the others out. I know that memory stayed with us longer than any other. The screams that we endured haunted us for the many months that followed.

CHAPTER 3
TABLE FOR SIX

The reality of what the Earth, as we had always known it, had become, was upon us. We six, three men and three women, the last living organisms on the face of this planet in what I knew as Project Dome. The rest of the Earth was a frozen solid ball of complete blackness. We could hardly imagine the scene beyond our walls where billions of people and animals were dead and frozen, thank God. Unless rescued, we six knew we would live our lives together in this dome until old age took us. There are no germs in our environment, no colds, no diseases, nothing would prematurely end our lives. This germ free living was the only way we could eliminate the need for hospitals and medicine.

Our computers supply synthetic water, and the

only sustenance required for our bodies. The latter is in pill form we would swallow once a day. The computers will keep supplying these capsules for as long as we could operate the computers. We will either have to be rescued by some other life form or we will become old and feeble and eventually unable to care for ourselves and each other.

There would be no procreating in Project Dome. The sterilization process we have to engage in before entering the dome not only eliminates any germs that would be carried in, but it also eliminates the capacity to reproduce, ever. At least this wasn't a moral decision that we were left to face. Should we bring new life into this bleak existence? I am fairly certain we would all have agreed not to reproduce, however, this subject was never debated. It was surely speculated about by all, but never discussed. It reminded us of our mortality.

We six weren't alone in Project Dome. We lived with fifteen robots. They carried out some of the simpler tasks required for the upkeep of the dome. These robots were capable of more complicated processes, meant for the larger population the dome was designed to house. We did not need the robots for much more than simple housekeeping and grounds maintenance. Nor did we interact with them much, for they were programmed to come out and tend to the grounds while the people slept.

Aside from the friends, strangers and God forgive us, family members that we'd kept out of the dome on that terrible day, I believe the one thing that weighed on our minds and contributed to our endless bouts with depression, was the fact that we would never eat solid food again.

One gray pill, once a day, was all that our bodies required to sustain life. A scientific miracle, yes, but an unintended torture nonetheless. I know the luxury of sitting down to a meal must have seemed trivial to the scientists who invented this singular life sustaining capsule, which, in turn, eliminated the need for food manufacture and storage. But while we endured months of dreary, meaningless existence, dreams of food governed our thoughts with more and more frequency. We knew our lives were over. It was simply a matter of time. There were no simple pleasures to look forward to aside from sex, and this too lost its ability to overcome the moment after a short time. We had no walks in the fresh air, no vacations or picnics to look forward to. There were no birds flying overhead, no barking dogs, no purring cats, no babies or small children to bring joy to our lives. We had nothing. Nothing but this circular dome, with six people existing inside and a black frozen nothingness outside, forever. Yet live on, we did, and we endured the same monotonous routine day in and day out for months. Or should I write, time in and time out, for we have no day or night? We have no sunrises or sunsets, no summer, spring, fall or winter. Only time. I know for myself, there were moments when I didn't think I could hold it together. I'm sure this had to be true for each of us. We had a library in the dome and one could read just about any book one could think of. But I found it made me more homesick for my old life. We could watch movies to fill some of the endless stretch of time, but the feelings we had when the movie was over are hard to describe. For there was nothing left, ever. No cars, no airplanes, no lakes, rivers, or creeks. No fishing or hunting or going out to dinner. No children, no ordinary life problems to solve. There certainly wasn't a need for money anymore. The magnitude of the loss we have experienced goes on and on. So why food and the desire to eat something was so prominent I can't understand. Only that it was.

CHAPTER 4
GREEN EGGS AND HAM

Thoughts of actual food consumed us. I guess there were many small luxuries of life we could have chosen for our thoughts to be consumed by, but I think this particular one chose us. That's the only explanation I can come up with. Our very existence was over and we couldn't think of much else except eating regular food. We had accepted the reality of our lives. Why couldn't we accept the fact that we would never have a solid meal again? We just couldn't, that's all. We talked about food in great detail, sharing everything from textures and colors to aromas and tastes. Looking back, I think these conversations helped to alleviate some cravings. We were being ridiculous, but we couldn't stop ourselves. I don't know that anyone will ever find us or read this journal, but I still have to write, for myself mostly. We found the answer to our dream. After endless months of a gray capsule swallowed once a day, one of us stumbled across a large crate marked experimental vegetable seeds. Why it was there, we can only speculate. Perhaps the scientists had anticipated the people's longing for real food. Perhaps they were to provide a more naturalistic environment within the dome, thus providing gardens and gardening for the people, maybe if only to occupy their time. We didn't care why they were there. All we cared about is that they were here and we had found them! We have artificial soil and grass and plants. These are almost like the real thing, genuine enough looking anyway, but yet not real. But the seeds were real, the product they could produce was real and finally we felt we had something to look forward to and live for.

We found them in the entryway. In the sort of closet type compartment on the other side of the sterilization chamber, a place that we had no reason to explore. They had sat here the whole time, just waiting to be discovered, planted, nurtured, harvested, and eaten. Yes, eaten. Our tortuous make believe food conversations took on a whole new meaning. We were fairly confident that the artificial soil could support and grow a real vegetable seed. The environment we lived in was constant and we felt virtually ideal for growing a garden. So, grow a garden we did. We selected one of everything in the crate. There were carrots, lettuce, broccoli, tomatoes, onions, peppers, and potatoes. A virtual smorgasbord of vegetable delights. We had already decided that we would let some vegetables go to seed so we could continue to have actual food for as long as we lived. In our minds, our existence finally had meaning, for we had a garden to grow.

We held our breaths in anticipation, waiting to see if the artificial soil could indeed produce a live plant. Our group felt certain that the synthetic water wouldn't harm them, for it didn't harm us, but the soil was another matter. We refused to believe that we had stumbled across these jewels only to have our hopes dashed from the soil not being able to support life. Our fears were unwarranted, we soon discovered. The emotions that the green mist of tiny seedlings poking their heads above the soil gave us were not unlike the feelings a mother has when she looks at her new baby. Of that I'm quite certain. We sat around our table fantasizing about our vegetarian feast that wasn't so very far off. During the waking hours, we laughed and joked with each other, something we hadn't done for quite some time. We tended to our seedlings and later full-grown plants. While we slept, we dreamed of our first actual meal. We disciplined ourselves not to pick the vegetables before they were ripe, not with complete success, but surprisingly well. We had agreed that in another week we would harvest. None of us slept well in anticipation. Talk of our garden filled our every waking moment. Personally, I had never cared much for vegetables. But the thought of getting to experience these jewels was unequaled to anything I had ever dreamed of in my entire life.

CHAPTER 5

1 ROBOT

What happened next, none of us had expected. As scientists, we should have, but we didn't. As I write in this journal, I weep at the memory of it. For during the so-called night of our damned domed existence, the robot maintenance crew leveled our beautiful, precious garden. Once it had happened, and we got over the initial shock, we realized it made perfect sense. For any foreign matter was removed while we slept by the meticulous care of the robots. I did not see often them because they only came out while we slept, or else we might have realized the potential threat and been able to save our exquisite and adored garden. Why they hadn't discovered it sooner, we weren't sure. For it definitely would have been less painful had they found it sooner. For we were less than a week away from harvest.

We felt defeated and depressed beyond belief. We all did nothing but lay in our bunks for days. The hopelessness of the reality of our situation lay heavy on our hearts. If someone could have told me a few years ago, or even a few months ago that a carrot, or lack of one, could have triggered such enormous emotions in me, I would have thought them insane, but it was real. After we wallowed in our misery for a few days, the verdict was unanimous; we would replant. This time we would watch our garden with the vigilance of a mother. We would rotate on all night shifts to keep a 24-hour watch on our children. Our precious tomatoes, onions, and peppers would reach maturity this time. We could interfere with the robots' work, but our fields of expertise didn't include re-programming the damn things. So we had no choice but to keep an ever-watchful eye on our babies. It turned out it was easy to intervene with the robots. We wished we had known before because we would have been eating by now if not for them. So now we had months to wait again. The good news was we had nothing else to do and nothing but time on our side.

CHAPTER 6
LET'S GET READY TO RUMBLE

I don't need to articulate the procedure again. Our hearts were in it because what else did we have to look forward to except our garden and the ever distant, much anticipated meal? But it was different this time. We were anxious and afraid instead of light-hearted and cheerful. So night after night for months we took turns rotating a night shift, ever diligent, and we could intervene when the robots came again.

Well, were we successful? Did we finally produce a garden that yielded a crop fit for a king? Did we finally get to enjoy our hearts' desire? Solid food? After months and months of waiting and then months and months of waiting again, did we get our payoff? Yes, we did. Our first meal was the most memorable, of course. We made absolute pigs of ourselves. We crunched and smacked and chewed, yes, chewed, carrots and broccoli and tomatoes and potatoes for hours. It was a little bit like heaven in the hell in which we lived. We ate until we were full, and then we kept eating, and then we ate some more. I think we were all eager to go to bed so as to wake up and have breakfast to look forward to. We all slept better that night than we had in a long, long time. The vegetables were delicious beyond belief. We all ended up throwing up and had bouts of terrible diarrhea, but we didn't care. Only after we recovered from our belly aches were we able to verbally reflect on our first great disappointment with the garden. We felt melancholy and deliciously full for the first time in a long while. We spent several months coming up with every vegetable recipe we could think of. Every combination of vegetables we could imagine, and we were truly content. While we had no cookware, because the gray pills replaced any need to cook anything. We came up with pots and vessels to cook in. Then we created a type of stove that produced heat enough to bake and fry and boil. It was sometime before we ran out of ideas with which to prepare our meals. We felt happy and had something to look forward to for a while. We mutually, painstakingly, avoided any talk of our actual dismal surroundings. It was wonderful to feel full of life and enjoying conversation with each other.

CHAPTER 7

DOWN WITH THE
SICKNESS

The happiness was to be relatively short-
lived. After about a month, the first signs
of sickness started showing up. At first, we
thought it was just our bodies trying to adjust to the
food that was being introduced into our systems. We
tried slowing down on our real food and only ate
every other day. On the off days, we took our gray
capsule. This seemed to help at first. But within
another month, three of us were dead. There was
nothing we could do. We had no doctors, no medicine. The three of us that were left didn't take time to
grieve. We were too busy trying to find the cause of
the sickness, which might tell us how to cure it. We
ran tests on everything, the water supply, the air
supply, the computer generated gray capsules, and we

came up with nothing. We looked for any irregularities in the dome itself, but still we came up with nothing. We knew if we had the same sickness as the other three that there wasn't much time left for us remaining. So we did the one thing we had hoped we wouldn't have to do. Our team ran tissue samples on our dead teammates. The computers told us something that our brains couldn't comprehend, that the tissue and ultimately the body had been killed by germs. Our pal, the sterilization chamber, takes out the immune system during its process, so even the common cold could kill us. But since we live in a completely germ-free environment, we need no immune system. Everything that comes through the chamber is freed of any germs, so how and where did these germs leak in, and from a frozen dead planet nonetheless, that had killed three of us?

CHAPTER 8

TIME IS ON MY SIDE

N ow, I'm the only one left alive, and I have little time. I'm hurrying to finish this journal before I too am dead. I'm quite certain I have figured it out. But I know it no longer really matters. You see, the one specific that we all overlooked and that dawned on me altogether too late was where we had actually found our precious crate of killer seeds. They were in storage on the outside of the sterilization chamber and, in our excitement; we didn't stop to spend the five life-saving minutes required to protect us from the germs they carried. Oh sure, I think I can step into the sterilization chamber, and all the germs that are living inside my body would be destroyed. I believe that could be the cure, and I could live on. But I don't think I'm going to try that. I would rather be dead than to live my life out alone in Project Dome.

So, in another day, two at the most, I too will be killed by the germs. And the human race will become extinct.

ABOUT THE AUTHOR

T. D. Chase is a native of Oregon. She has a B.S. in Psychology from Southern Oregon University.

Tamara believes in paying it forward and that Karma is alive and well.

She lives with her fiancé, Thomas, and they share their home with nine rescued fur babies.

When she's not writing books or tending to animals, Tamara enjoys riding her Harley Davidson.

ALSO BY T. D. CHASE

SELF HELP BOOKS

Setting Personal Boundaries

Manifesting

FICTION

Project Dome

Made in the USA
Las Vegas, NV
17 October 2023